THE FUTURE GOD OF LOVE

DILMAN DILA

LUNA NOVELLA #4

Text Copyright © 2021 Dilman Dila
Cover © 2021 Jay Johnstone

First published by Luna Press Publishing, Edinburgh, 2021

The Future God of Love ©2021. All rights reserved. No part of this publication may be reproduced, stored in a retrieval system, or transmitted in any form or by any means, electronic, mechanical, photocopy, recording or otherwise, without prior written permission of the copyright owners. Nor can it be circulated in any form of binding or cover other than that in which it is published and without similar condition including this condition being imposed on a subsequent purchaser.

www.lunapresspublishing.com
ISBN-13: 978-1-913387-51-8.

To Lisa, who does not want a story for her birthday.

Contents

Chapter One	1
Chapter Two	13
Chapter Three	23
Chapter Four	36
Chapter Five	47
Chapter Six	57
Chapter Seven	67

Chapter One

Jamaaro sat on a soft, cow-skin mat, staring idly at a moth as it danced around a tadooba flame. Only a little oil remained in the lamp and it emitted more soot than light, filling his hut with a faint smell of onions. The oil can sat on a bookshelf at the other end of the room, yet he could not summon energy to refill the tadooba. He saw himself as a wounded rooster, lying in the yard, waiting for a knife – *her voice* – to slice his neck. The voice would come from wang oo, where elders had gathered to hear her audition for resident storyteller. The breeze rattled the half-open window, and murmurs filtered in. The elders were already excited, though her show had not begun. He overheard one giving her a pet name, Nyadwe, the daughter of the moon, for she was so, so beautiful. Another claimed that she had a captivating voice that made people float above the world like happy birds. A third elder said she was such a gifted storyteller that she did not need an actor to narrate her story, nor did she need musicians and dancers and performers. She did it all by herself, relying on her voice. That enchanting voice.

"Kwaro sent her to be the laboki of Wendo town," one

elder said, raising his voice to make sure Jamaaro could hear him. The others fell silent for a moment, as if waiting for Jamaaro's response, and then they continued praising Nyadwe.

A long time ago, after his breakout story, elders had said that kwaro had blessed him with a rare gift, and so they made him the new laboki even though the resident storyteller was doing well. But they were saying this of her even before she auditioned, and he knew it was because he had failed to give them any good story for the last thirty moons.

He wanted to hate her for she would take away his job, but he was thankful that the ancestors had sent someone to put him out of his misery. He would not have to suffer anymore, to create a new story every full moon, for it would now be her duty. The town needed a new story regularly for stories kept the darkness away, stories made them to remember what life had been like yesterday, and to imagine what life would be like tomorrow. Stories were spiritual food and the town was starving. They survived on his old stories, eating and regurgitating and eating them in a desperate loop, but these could not give them new dreams. They supplemented this stale diet by borrowing stories from other towns, but to be happy they needed stories set in Wendo, with characters unique to their town.

Without any *new* and *good* stories, the town would die.

If he was an ordinary laboki, they would already have gotten rid of him. He was a future god, and this helped to keep the town alive for it made his stale stories palatable.

He became a future kwaro when he was still a boy, just as his beard had started to sprout. At that time he was struggling through a traumatic childhood and was not even thinking about being a laboki. He feared he would end up a drunkard like his father, or hopeless like his elder brother, who killed himself because he could not afford dowry to marry. Though at that time Jamaaro still had a few seasons before he could think of marriage, he worried that no woman would want to be his wife because he could not afford bridal wealth.

He had begun to imagine what love would be like if there was no bride price. Would people still put a price on everything? Would fathers treat their daughters like cattle, and would wedding ceremonies still be some kind of slave markets? He then created a story, Children of the Wound, in which he painted his vision of marriage. He first performed it at a market, hoping for nothing more than a few cowrie shells to buy himself lunch, but his performance captivated the entire market and the rwot invited him to audition. Once he told the story properly, with music and dance and animated images, people begun to dream of the world he had imagined. Within a few moons, bride price was outlawed and weddings ceased being markets. If any dowry was involved, it was a gift that the groom's family gave as they pleased and as they could afford.

The universal success of the story secured him a high status as a kwaro of love. Upon his death, they would build shrines in his honour. People would worship him and ask him to bless their love affairs and their marriages. His name was already important in marriage rituals, and his songs had become a central part of courtship dances and weddings.

And yet, he never found anyone to love him.

He sometimes blamed it on the pressure to create a new story every full moon, to give people new histories, new memories, new meanings in their lives. To keep the town dreaming happy dreams. He had done so well until he burned out. Now he could not produce anything good anymore, and it was killing the town. People were having less and less beautiful dreams, and some had begun to complain of nightmares. Worse, some people were having blank sleeps with no dreams, as if they were dead. Fewer birds flew to their forests, and they had not seen butterflies or bees in a while. Festivities were dull, almost as if every gathering was a funeral, for a thick mist of unhappiness hung over their town. Already, since the last full moon, two families had migrated.

They needed a new storyteller.

Just as two rwot could not rule at the same time, two laboki could not serve the same town simultaneously. Legend had it that a great town once had more than one laboki, and every market day, which happened every eight days, they consumed a new story. The town was happy and prosperous and full of beautiful dreams until its laboki started to compete. When one created a story that inspired people to build bigger granaries, another would encourage them to eat all harvest at once. Chaos set in, civil war broke out, and since then no town hosted more than one resident storyteller.

He wanted to hate this Nyadwe for he still wanted to tell stories. It was the only thing he knew, and the only way he overcame loneliness. He would die if he could not do it anymore. He could not become a farmer or mechanic. He did not know how to idle under a tree and drink banana wine all day. He needed to keep working. Some part of him hoped that she would turn out like others. They came burning with ambition but turned out to be mediocre copycats.

And yet he thought that maybe it was time for him to retire. He had to think of a new life. His beards were going grey, his hair was thinning, and his belly was growing bigger, yet he was still a virgin. He had not even ever had a girlfriend. Maybe now he would find time to socialise, to learn how to talk to women. Maybe then he would fall in love.

Maybe. Just maybe.

The oil ran out. The flame waned, and the gloom tightened itself around him. The moth fled out of the window, seeking happiness elsewhere. The scent of the burning wick stung his nose. Still, he did not refill the tadooba. He stared at it until the wick glowed red and darkness settled in the hut. A beam of moonlight flowed in through the window and fell on the floor, creating a spot of blue just near his feet.

He became aware that the murmur of the elders had died down. He stiffened, his eyes opened wider, so wide that he could make out the silhouette of his easel. He spent all his time with it, so much time that he thought of it as his wife, as his only friend. It had helped him make all drawings for pictures were essential to every tale, more important than the music, the poetry, the dancing and the performers. People needed to see what he imagined and only then could their dreams be wild and beautiful.

He listened for Nyadwe's voice, but a deep silence flowed out of wang oo. He thought Nyadwe already had the image-wheel turning, animating her drawings, and that her first pictures were already showing to the audience. That's how all stories started. With moving pictures. If it was good, the audience would cheer and clap. If bad, they would boo. If they did not know what to make of it, they would stay silent.

Like now. No cheers, no boos. Exactly how they had greeted the first image in Children of the Wound; a little girl with a pot on her head and a basket in one hand. A horned snake peeping out of the basket while a horned parrot sitting on the lip of the pot. No one had known what to expect from an image that mixed reality with fantasy.

He waited to hear the song that would accompany the moving pictures. Nothing. No drum, no harp, no flute. Just a voice. A voice so sweet that for a moment he thought she was singing. It sounded like the humming olit bird that seduced the sun into rising every morning. It was a living thing and it sailed in through his window, upon the moonbeams, and swirled around him like mist. He shuddered. He wanted to hear it every day, for the rest of his life.

He had created a story that changed marriage, but he had never gotten married. He was a future god of love, but he had never known love. He wished success had come to him later in life, after his first taste of a woman's love, but it had come so early, and it had made him arrogant. He was a future god and he needed a woman fit enough to be a goddess. Not just in beauty, but what came out of them. He wanted her to help him create better stories, to give him the emotional support he needed to create, to lift his spirit when he was low. Like now. He did not want a wife. He wanted a muse.

That voice…

Why was there no song?

The story was about a girl and her parents. Jamaaro frowned. What a commonplace story, he thought. How could a voice so strong tell a story so weak?

Weak? No, there was something about that tale, something

that made him stand up and lean against the window to catch every word. He could not see the pavilion on which she stood. He could only see a small portion of the audience, listening attentively to a story about raising a little girl. The father never lifted a finger against her, but the mother, oh she did give the little girl a few good slaps, and this shaped her into a good girl, now a rwot who would lead her people to a great, great destiny.

Jamaaro's fingers gripped the windowsill so tight that it hurt. His jaws clenched. A simple story. Well told. A moving story. Though the audience was not clapping, though there was no song and dance and fanfare, a moving story. Now, he saw why his craft had stagnated. Children of the Wound was so endearing because everyone could relate to it. He should have stuck to telling simple stories like that. He should not have started dreaming up grand fantasies set in worlds that no one understood.

Her story would travel wide, rewriting histories, rewriting memories, illustrating how parents should behave; that fathers should be gentle and caring and should never beat their children, and that a mother's tough love makes a child a better person. A simple narrative, with a powerful message. He should have created things like that.

Jamaaro rushed out of the hut, anxious not to miss the rest of the story. As he approached wang oo, he noticed that the crowd was restless. Wang oo was an open space in the centre of the town, big enough to accommodate all of its seven thousand residents. However, this being an audition rather than a storytelling night, only about two hundred elders had gathered. They sat on small stools in a semi-circle around a fire, facing the storyteller, who stood on a raised pavilion with the image-wheel beside her. It was blank, no drawings with glow-in-the-dark stones. There were no musicians either, no dancers, no performers.

How could this be a story? His first performance in the market, though he had not had images, had used song and dance and puppets. How could this woman rely only on her voice?

The rwot stood up and walked away, muttering something about it all being a waste of time. She opened a deluge. People walked away, one at a time, taking their stools with them, until wang oo was empty. Nyadwe continued to speak, as if she still had an audience. Now, musicians in a nearby bar kicked up a racket. They always respected performances so as not interfere, but they must have already gotten wind of her flop.

She continued to talk for a moment, her voice falling on his ears like music, her eyes fixed on him like warm moons in a cold night. His knees trembled, his fingers clasped tight together, lips pressed tight. How could the elders not see the beauty of the story? How could they not feel the power of this simple story?

She was beyond beautiful. The firelight fell on one side of her face, painting it red, and the moonlight fell on the other side, painting it blue, giving her the beauty of a goddess.

His goddess.

He had fallen in love with her voice, with her storytelling, and seeing her made his heart melt and opened up a hollowness in his stomach. Here was the woman he had been waiting for all his life.

She paused her story and looked at him, as though just

noticing him.

"You don't have to stay," she said. "I'll talk to the grass."

I like your story, he wanted to say. His throat was dry. He could not take his eyes off her. The fire crackled.

"I'm not really a storyteller," she said. "Please go away."

"You are," he heard a voice. He looked around to see who else was there, for surely those words had not come from him.

"Am I?" she said. "You are just being kind," she added after a pause.

He wanted to describe the feelings her story had stirred up in him. He wanted to tell her about the moment that he had realised what kind of stories he should create. The words could not come out. He looked around again, hoping to see that stranger that had spoken on his behalf, praying to kwaro that the stranger would speak again.

"Let me buy you a drink," the voice said. He knew that voice, it was one of his characters, the hero in Children of the Wound. Jamaaro looked around, hoping to catch sight of this person, who he had modelled after his dead brother, but he could only see the fireflies that suddenly took flight.

The moment passed. A long moment. He felt stupid for asking her out. It could not be his character, he realised, for he would have known exactly what to say, he would have known how to properly court a woman.

Why would she want to be his goddess anyway?

Outside Wendo, people knew nothing about him, but in the town they knew exactly who he was. They knew that underneath that status of a future kwaro, he was a dirty motherless boy with a drunkard for a father. She was a stranger in town, but since she was staging an audition, he thought she had been around for over four days. She surely would have heard about him, that he was a 'difficult' person, a 'weird' person, that he liked staying alone and that he refused to let anyone love him. What woman would want such a man?

"You?" she said, giggling. "Buy me a drink?"

She knows, he thought. After he died his spirit would join the ranks of kwaro, but for now it was stuck in a motherless son of a drunkard, in the brother of a suicide, in a stinking boy who lived in a cave like a wild animal. They did not love *him*. They loved his *spirit*.

He stood there feeling stupid. He should have offered to mentor her. Maybe, over time of them working together, she would come to love that son of a drunkard. She would see that the cave boy was kind and gentle and had a great heart. Over time, she would accept his invitation for a drink, and eventually to marry him. He should have offered to be her teacher.

He wanted to walk away, to run back into his hut and bury himself under the cow-hide mat, and he hated himself that he could not break away from the spell she had cast over him.

Giggling, she jumped off the pavilion and, like a playful girl, skipped up to him. She stopped a pace away, a smile on her face. She did not have dimples, and yet her smile set his blood on fire. A smile that had been made just for him.

"Why do you want to hang out with me?" she said.

He used to imagine he was tall, and most women only reached his chest, but she was almost his height. He thought she was about half his age. She looked so young that she probably had recently 'visited the bush', the ritual every girl underwent to transition into adulthood.

"You," he said, his voice quivering. "You, uhm, you are…." He trailed off. He wished he could summon one of his characters to talk for him.

"Beautiful?" she said. "Gorgeous? Stunning? Lovely?" She chuckled, but now he could not detect derision in her voice. Just a playfulness, a teasing tone. "I've heard it all and I know that look on your face. You are not the first man to fall in love with me at first sight."

He bit his lips hard. *I liked your story*, he wanted to insist. *I'm not like other men who fall for you because of your beauty*, he wanted to explain. *I'm different. I'm a future god. I saw the inside of you, I saw your worth and I want you to be my goddess.* In his head the words came out eloquently, and swept her off her feet, and she hugged him and gave him a kiss. In her eyes he saw the moon, shinning bright.

"Did you really like my story or was that a pick up line?" she said.

"I like," he stammered. His legs itched to run away, and he dug deep inside him to find courage to say the thing that he should have said to her. "You are – uhm – teach you."

"What?"

"I can teach you."

"Teach me?"

He nodded. "You can be a good storyteller with proper training." He was surprised that he had said that much, and it left him breathless and enervated.

"So you are a storyteller?" she said.

He nodded. *I'm the future god of love*, he wanted to add, but only swallowed hard. Had she not recognised him? His images were commonplace. In the rwot's palace, where she had to get a go ahead for the audition, his statue stood in the front lawn and there was a drawing of him smiling on one wall. Maybe she did not recognise him because of the lights. Maybe, by the time she did, she would see that he was more than just the son of a drunkard.

She was quiet for a long moment. The smile never left her face, and her eyes stayed on his. He could not hold her stare, could not stand the glare of the moon in her pupils. He looked at the fire burning beside the pavilion like a lonely ghost hungry for companionship.

"Fair enough," she finally said. "You are too shy to pick up a woman you have just met, so well, maybe you saw something in my story that those elders didn't see."

He nodded again, vigorously. He thought his neck would snap.

"Okay then," she said. "Let's go get drunk and see if we fall in love."

Drunk? He had never gotten drunk, but now he knew what it felt like.

She took his hand and a hot sensation spread throughout his body. Her hands were soft, small and fragile. She pressed her body close to his, and he wanted to melt into her. When she started to drag him toward the bar, he could not resist.

Chapter Two

They walked down a sandy path and he was aware of only one thing; her hand on his, hot as a stove. Sweat gathered under his shirt. It was made of fine bark-cloth, and was light enough to allow the breeze to soothe him, yet it could not stop the deluge of sweat. He panicked, afraid she would take her hand away once his became disgustingly moist. They walked in silence, sand crunching under their feet, his heart beating so loud that he could not hear the music from the bar they were heading to. In his daze, he did not pay much attention to it until they arrived. Akela's Kafunda.

No, not that bar! He wanted to tell her. Not Akela's Kafunda!

He swallowed hard to get rid of molten rocks in his throat. He would have preferred Mama Mapengo's joint, which was much further away. Then, he would prolong the moment of walking with her, hands locked, and he would avoid Akela.

Let's keep walking, he tried to say.

She gave him a smile, and skipped off the road onto Akela's driveway, dragging him. He could not resist. Akela would tell her who he was, and then they would not get drunk together.

Then, she would not fall in love with him.

The kafunda had a porous bamboo wall, which gave it an open-air feel and kept it cool, and a domed glass-slat roof, through which they could see the sky. The enclosure was designed to resemble a courtyard with two huts in the middle, where they brewed all sorts of alcohols. Sweet slow music engulfed them, just as if the song was a cloud they had walked into. Three musicians sat on a pavilion at one end. One blew a cow-horn flute, another strummed an adungo, and the third worked a long drum. Their tunes flowed out of pot-speakers, which were placed around the wall. Patrons sat on small stools, encircling pots from which they sucked ajono using long tubes. A lamp, suspended on thin wire such that they looked like hovering lights, glowed above each beer circle.

In the past, the bar would have been packed on such a full moon night. After the show in wang oo, people would have moved into the various bifunda spread all over town for more shows, where the new story he had just created would be retold with much festivities. This night a general aura of sadness hung upon the town, for it had been a long time since he had created a story that really excited everyone. Her flop worsened the mood, for now everyone was afraid that it would be a while before they got a replacement laboki. Of the twenty beer circles, only four were occupied, each with about six people only.

She dragged him to one of the smallest circles, with only four stools, and pushed away two in case someone was tempted to join them. She also removed three tubes from the pot, and Jamaaro saw that she wanted to share one with him. He did not know how to react to that.

She sat on a stool, pulled the other so close and patted it while giving him a big smile. He sat, moving as if a strange power was in total control of his body. Once he was seated, she again took hold of his hand and gave it a squeeze. She sucked ajono, then passed the tube to him. He had never liked millet beer, and on the few occasions that he drank he opted for banana wine, but her lips flavoured the tube and he sucked with great relish.

Then Akela came out of one of the brewing huts. She carried a large calabash of hot water and walked straight to their circle. Even from the distance, Jamaaro could see the expression on her face and it rubbed away some of his happiness.

"Ha," Akela said as she poured hot water into the beer pot, noticing that he was holding hands with the strange woman. "The future kwaro of love finally finds love."

Jamaaro felt as though she had poured the hot water on his face. He gritted his teeth.

"Oh," she said. "It's you?"

He wanted to punch Akela. Now this beautiful woman knew there was something wrong with him, that he was unable to make friends, unable to enjoy human companionship, unable to find love and raise a decent family. That he was not the kind of man to fall in love with.

She wriggled her hand to disentangle it from his, and he felt the burning sensation of rejection where their skin had touched.

"I'm with Jamaaro, the future kwaro of love?" She spoke in a near whisper, her eyes, full of wonder, drilling holes into his skull.

Jamaaro could not stand the stare. He suddenly felt the weight of his loneliness. She would not want him, not anymore. She now knew that he was just a motherless boy who lived in a cave with a drunkard father, a dirty little boy.

"Careful with him," Akela said. "He fears love." She chuckled, and it sounded like a jeer.

Akela emptied the calabash and walked away, her sandals slapping too loudly against the floor. Jamaaro kept his eyes on the pot. Akela had been his first encounter with love, a long time ago just after he had managed to secure a cleaning job at a mechanic's shop. Her mother was a baker and Akela would bring kabalagala to sell in the workshop. She always gave him one for free. After several moons, she asked him if he enjoyed the pancakes, and he gave her a bland yes. She asked if he wanted to eat one for the rest of his life, and he said, "No, they'll make me fat." He had wanted it to come out as a joke, but he saw the pain on her face, and after all this time he could still hear her slippers slapping the ground as she ran away. It later occurred to him that she was not really talking about kabalagala. By then, it was a little too late. She was already married.

Her marriage failed, however, and he found courage to ask if she still made kabalagala. By then he had found success as a storyteller and he was thinking of a wife. Her eyes had grown red in fury. "If you had loved me back," she had said, "I'd not have ended up with a monster."

Her face still had scars from that marriage. She killed her husband when he tried to force her back into his home, and the rwot banished her from Wendo. She fled before her in-laws could kill her in revenge. Inspired by her tale, Jamaaro created a story about a woman who marries a shape-shifting monster, a handsome man in the day and a hyena in the night. The story moved the rwot to pardon her, and her in-laws to make peace with her. It rewrote the history of violence in intimate relationships, and many towns created family watch groups to deter gender violence. It upheld his status as a future kwaro of love.

He looked at Akela until she vanished in the hut, and he wondered what his life would have been like if he had been intelligent enough to decipher the meaning of kabalagala. Would he have ended up a future kwaro, or would marriage have killed his ability to create stories?

"She was once my muse," Jamaaro heard someone say.

He jumped, and looked up at Nyadwe, who was still staring at him wide-eyed. He hoped she had not heard his confession. He had never told anyone about his relationship with Akela.

"I came here to find you," Nyadwe said, her voice still low, almost a whisper.

Jamaaro did not know how to react. He thought she was saying it simply because Akela had said his name, but she could easily take advantage of him since love-at-first-sight had made him a fool, and she knew it, so why would she say something like that? And if she really came to Wendo to find him, she would have recognised him at once.

"Really," she said, as if reading his confusion. "I came here to find you."

"A mentor?" he said. "I alr–"

"No." She interrupted. "I'm not a storyteller and I don't want a mentor."

He now looked at her, completely at a loss of what to make

of her. He thought she would elaborate, but she instead took the tube and sucked beer, long and hard, as if the conversation had come to an end.

"Why are you looking for me?" he said.

"I told the rwot I'm a storyteller because I didn't want her to know exactly why I came," she said. "She must be so desperate for a laboki that she didn't even bother to check me out."

For a moment, he thought she was just being modest, like he had been. When they had offered him to audition, he had insisted he was just a dirty boy looking for his next meal. He only considered to audition after the rwot offered him free meals. He did not know what to offer her so she could accept her calling, but he was sure she had it in her, that gift of telling stories.

"You didn't recognise me," he said. "If you were looking for me, you'd know me."

She gave him a small smile. "Sorry, I first heard about you yesterday but one."

A small groan escaped his throat. How could she have not heard of him? His songs were played at every wedding. His stories were performed in every town's wang oo during the kwango-jogi festival, which was supposed to thank kwaro for a good harvest, but which had become synonymous with courtship. His images were in every village, every town, every palace. For her to claim that she had never heard of him was like saying she had never seen a sunrise.

"I come from far away," she said.

"Far away?" he said, feeling foolish for repeating her words. "Where?"

"You've never heard of my country," she said. And then added, rather too quickly, "I was in Kaliko when someone said you can help me, and that's the first time I heard of your name."

Kaliko was a village in a town half a day's flight away. If she had been there just two days ago, it could only mean she was hardly a day old in Wendo, and the rwot giving her an audition right away only emphasised the town's desperation.

"I'm looking for a song," she said. "The man in Kaliko said you can help me find it."

Me? He wanted to ask. How?

"A song?" he said.

She nodded, and sucked on the tube. "A very old song," she said.

"Why?" he said.

"Don't you want to know what the song is?" she said.

"Why are you looking for it?"

"It goes like this." She tried to sing, but the tune did not come. "I forget it," she said, her lips turning downward in pretend frustration. "I forget the beat. I can't remember the song."

"Then how will you find it?" he said.

"I know the lyrics," she said. "Nyalisa oh Nyalisa, I'm fed up of your wandering. You left me alone. You left me alone with the children. You go wandering all over the world. Why, why, why. Nyalisa Oh Nyalisa, I'm fed up of your wandering. Come back home."

She pushed the tube toward him. He hesitated, and then took it and sucked. The taste of her lips was stronger than ever on the tube, and it flavoured the warm beer that gushed down his throat, sweet and mushy. Akela was a good brewer. He wondered if she still made pancakes.

"Only you can help me find it," she said.

"Only me?"

He let go of the tube. She took it and sucked.

"You are a future kwaro of love. That makes you the only person able to help me."

"By finding this song?"

"Yes."

"How will I find it?"

"I don't know, but we'll have to travel the whole world looking for it."

We? The idea of travelling the world with her sent his heart into a crazy spin, and he feared it would collapse, for it had already been through too much drama in a short time.

"The whole world?" He took the tube from her and he sucked the beer.

"You'll have to abandon your home and become a vagrant for many seasons until we find it. We'll move from village to village, searching, until we find it."

She made it seem like a romantic adventure he might have created, in which two strangers go on a very long road trip to find a song that probably did not exist, but putting it in a story sense knocked him out of his daze. None of his characters would just drop everything and run away with a stranger. They would need a motivation far stronger than love at first sight. They would need to know the woman, and yet he did not even know her name.

"If I don't find the song," she said. "I'll die."

"We'll all die," he said.

"No," she said. "My spirit will wither into nothingness."
"Oh," he said. "Why?"

"That's what my father said on his deathbed," she said. "I must find the song if I'm to become an ancestor."

A sad smile appeared on her face. He noticed that she had a beard, a single strand of hair growing out of her chin, a bit of hair in front of her ears, like a shy side-burn, and the ghost of a moustache, a dark line on her upper lip that for a moment he thought was painted on. It made her even more beautiful and he knew he was hopelessly in love.

Saving a spirit from death was a strong enough motivation, he thought. His characters would certainly go out of their way to make sure someone served as an ancestor.

He thought about his life in the town, the dreariness of waking up every day, creating yet another banal story that people would forget in a few moons, seeing the same things, doing the same things, every day. Hearing the same whispers all the time, people saying that there is something wrong with him, that the future kwaro of love cannot find love. He thought about the pressure piling up on him to keep the town alive and how it had destroyed his social life.

"I don't even know your name," he said.

He felt her eyes on him, and he looked up to see a light twinkling in her pupils. She put a hand on his shoulder, and it caused an earthquake in his chest.

"My name is Nyalisa," she said.

"Nyalisa." He savoured the way it rolled off his tongue. "That's the name in the song."

She nodded. "The song is about me," she said.

He frowned. "You said it's an old song," he said.

She nodded again. "My mother named me after the song," she said, and from the way she stuttered, he thought she was lying. "I don't know why, so don't ask me, but the song is about me and if I don't find it my spirit will die."

"Tell me the truth," he said.

She was quiet for a long moment, and he thought he saw tears in her eyes.

"I can't," she said.

"Then how will I help you if I don't know the truth?" he said.

"I don't even know if Nyalisa is my real name," she said.

The silence stretched, and it was so deep he could not hear the music.

"I don't want to die," she said. A tear slipped down her cheek. "Please, help me."

Chapter Three

For the first time in many seasons, Jamaaro did not suffer insomnia. He slept like an enchanted log, and he dreamed about a girl with a beard, a single strand of hair that had pearls of ice coated with honey and cream. It was a wonderful dream until he awoke. Then, the smile he had had throughout his sleep vanished.

Yamo! He thought, sitting up with a jolt. *She's a yamo!*

Nothing else could explain the dream. The ancestors were warning him about her, but if she was a yamo, why was he still alive? Why had she not eaten him?

The window had stayed open to keep the hut cool, and now a strong beam of sunlight bounced off the wall and lit up the room with an orange glow. He looked at everything with a new sense, the mats and their colourful cushions, the stools, the shelves full of his works, the easel that had become his only friend and family, the harp and the drums and the flutes with which he made music, the rack full of his clothing. All scattered about in such a mess that it looked more like a studio than a bedroom. His bed felt incredibly big. He had made it just after his first success, when he could afford metal springs and soft-skin mattresses, and he had made it big enough for two people, imagining that he would have a wife within a few seasons. But, somehow, he had never even had a girlfriend and the bed accentuated his loneliness.

Yamo look like beautiful women with beards.

He had nearly brought her back home. She had told him that she did not have a place to spend the night, and he had struggled to find courage to ask her to come home with him. Then the moment had passed and she had said she would go to the inn where she had spent the previous night. Now, he thought that his cowardice had saved him for if he had brought her back home, she would have eaten him.

No, no, no, he said to himself. *She can't be a yamo.*

He slipped off of the bed and hurried out of the room. The hut was a perfect circle with a wall running across its diameter. One half had two bedrooms. If he had a family, he would have used one bedroom with his wife while the young children would have occupied the other. He however slept and worked in one and had turned the other into a store. He now ran into the store and rummaged through messy piles of books, searching for one about yamo. They were not a very common creature, and there were more myths than truths about them, but this book had an accurate description.

He found it, a green book with thin leaves that seemed fragile, covered in dust. The drawings were beautiful and surreal.

A hangover made him dizzy. Though he had not gotten drunk, he had taken in more alcohol than he usually consumed in a whole moon and it made him nauseous. With the book in one hand, he went to the outer room, the ddiiro, which took up the second half of the hut. If he had a family he would have passed the time here with his wife and children, eating meals, conversing, and he would have received visitors in it. Most families only had cushions and mats in this room. He had turned one part into the bathroom by setting up a glass cubicle with a tap and the other part into a kitchen, which had a shelf built into the wall. The bottom row of the shelf had two pots, a plate, a cup, a gourd, and a calabash. The middle row had foods and fruits, while the top row had broken utensils. A sun-stone stove stood under the shelf, glowing a dull yellow for it had been a few days since he had last put it out in the sun to charge. It had enough heat to boil a hibiscus drink, which he sipped as he read the book.

It confirmed that she was not a yamo.

Those demons liked to masquerade as very beautiful women, but they had very long goatee beards that they could not get rid of, whatever form they shape-shifted into. Sometimes they took the form of men and then they did not have to hide the goatee, but then, they would not easily get victims. It was easier to lure men with the promise of sex, so they hid their beard between their breasts and they wore clothing and jewellery that covered up their chin. Nyalisa had worn a simple wrap-around cloth that left the top of her breasts and her shoulders bare. She did not have a real beard, just that one strand of hair on her chin, which was not out of the ordinary. The book also said that when a person dreamed about yamo, the goatee was prominent and a greenish smoke swirl out of it, not pearls of ice coated with honey and cream.

He put the book down with a sigh, thanking kwaro for sending her his way. She was not a yamo. She was the goddess he had been waiting for all his life.

He finished the hibiscus drink and hurried into the bathroom, cleaned his teeth using a mswaki, had a bath, then rushed into the bedroom to pack. He could not imagine life without the easel so it was the first thing he would take. Once folded up it was no bigger than a large food tray. He considered taking his adungu, but the harp had no sentimental value and he could pick one up in any market along the way. He did not need that excess baggage. He had five incomplete works, one of which was nearly done, and since he had a compulsive obsession to finish stories, he had to take all five. If he left them behind, he would return to complete them. He packed them in a creation box along with a tune-maker where he stored samples of unfinished songs. Then, he stuffed some clothes into a bag.

He gave the room one last look. Would he miss anything?

Other than the cave, this was the only home he had ever known, and yet, like the cave, it had never really felt like a home. It takes more than one person to turn a hut into a home.

He walked out dragging the creation box, the bag of clothes slung over his shoulder and the easel tucked under his armpit. He paused at the doorway, aware it was the last time he was walking out of this hut.

The sun had climbed a little higher, already fierce. If he had a family, he would have had many huts in his boma, but only one stood lonely in the middle of a vast courtyard, which was overgrown with daffodils and hibiscus shrubs, making it look like a hut in a bush. The hedge was however neatly trimmed for the neighbours tended them. Children made a racket in a boma to his left, while the neighbours to his right sung a song to worship an ancestor. He picked his way through the weeds to the backyard, where a bruka sat on a stone slab. It was oval shaped, with thin bird-like legs, and eagle-like wings sticking on its top. He rarely used it.

An old man was sweeping the wang oo, puffs of dust blowing around him. They called him Oywetch, which meant 'the broom'. Jamaaro had never seen him without the broom, even in the middle of the night when he was not sweeping, he clutched it tight in his palm. Every wang oo had such a creature, a spirit in the shape of an old man with a broom stuck in his hand, whose only job was to clean the place where the town's dreams came alive.

Oywetch waved. Jamaaro waved back, wondering if he would ever exchange greetings with him again. It had become part of his morning ritual and now it felt like a goodbye. He had decided not to tell anyone about his departure, not the rwot and not any of the elders. They would know after a day that he was not coming back.

"I greet you," Oywetch said, his eyes settling briefly on the bag and the packed easel, his lips trembling slightly as if they wanted to add something.

"Eh yii," Jamaaro replied. "How did you sleep?"

"Ah fine," Oywetch said. "I've never seen you smile before."

Jamaaro, in panic, pursed his mouth. "I'm not smiling," he said.

"I heard you fell in love last night," Oywetch said, again glancing at the bag.

Jamaaro felt the weight of the sun on his face, his brain

beginning to boil. A sudden silence engulfed the world, the worshiping neighbours stopped singing and the children stopped playing, as if everyone awaited his reply. Were they laughing at him for falling in love with a stranger? Were they saying that only a desperate man would think that any girl who smiled with him had fallen for him?

The old man walked closer to hedge, dragging the broom such that a trail of dust followed him. He stopped just on the other side, giving Jamaaro a big smile.

"She's a pretty one," Oywetch said.

"I'm not smiling," Jamaaro said.

"Listen to my old tongue," Oywetch said. "Why is it only you enjoyed her story?"

Had he been listening last night? The wang oo was a wide-open space and there had been no one within earshot when he had talked to Nyalisa, but Oywetch was a spirit.

"I didn't enjoy her story," Jamaaro said, his jaws pressing each other tight.

"You can't hide things from these old ears," Oywetch said.

Jamaaro wanted to jump into the bruka and fly away, to hurry to the love waiting for him at a riverside, yet the old man's words sunk deep. Indeed, why had no one else enjoyed the story? He was a very harsh critic, even of his own works. He could not remember any story that had completely swept him off his senses. Why did hers, which was like gossip you would hear in the market?

Something had taken away his power of reason.

"Her voice," Oywetch said. "It's not human."

Jamaaro felt a tightening in his chest, his jaws clenched, his fingers dug into the easel. The bag felt heavy on his shoulder, threatening to drag him down into the weeds. Not human. That could explain everything. *I came here to find you.* She had enchanted him and, maybe, to throw him off guard, she had pretended not to recognise him.

"She's not yamo," he said, a little short of breath, voice quivering.

"Ah," Oywetch said. "So you have thought about it."

She enchanted you, a voice whispered. *She's using you.* But why?

He wanted to leave Wendo and she was a perfect excuse. Sooner or later, he would have had to pack his bags and hit the road to unknown worlds for there was nothing left for him in Wendo. She was just a catalyst. It would have been different if she were yamo, but she was not. Whatever she was, he could take care of himself.

"Work hard today," he said, and turned away from the old man.

"You work hard too," Oywetch said. "May kwaro bless your labour."

Jamaaro hurried to the bruka, thinking he had heard the last from the old man, but as he threw the door open, Oywetch spoke again.

"I know about the song she seeks," he said.

Jamaaro's fingers tightened on the cold metal of the bruka. He wanted to jump in and fly away, for if he knew about the song he would lose his resolve. He might never get another motivation to leave and he would stay stuck in the village for the rest of his life, lonely and miserable. Human or not, he liked something about her, and he wanted to find out where this new door opened to.

He jumped into the bruka, and released the fly-gear and he

pedalled. The wings started to flap, slow, slow, and then faster as he pedalled harder. But then, he could not ignore it. He had to know what the old man knew. He flipped the gear lock and the pedal clicked into stiff mode and the wings stopped flapping. He jumped out of the bruka and hurried back to the fence, where Oywetch still stood, patient, broom in hand, a wry smile smudging his wrinkles.

"How do you know about the song?" Jamaaro said.

"She doesn't keep it a secret," Oywetch said.

Jamaaro waited for him to say more, but Oywetch turned around and walked away.

"So you won't tell me?" Jamaaro said.

"I can't," Oywetch said, his broom scratching the ground too loudly.

"Then why did you bring it up?" Jamaaro said.

"To let you know she's not human," Oywetch said, still walking away.

Jamaaro stood at the fence for a long moment, not sure what to do, and Oywetch started to sweep the ground, dust rising in puffs around him. The sun streamed through the dust clouds, painting them a bright gold.

Jamaaro jumped over the fence, trotted to the old man, and snatched the broom so suddenly that Oywetch did not have a chance to resist.

Oywetch's eyes opened wide in horror. He looked at the broom in Jamaaro's hands, and then at his own palms, which oozed blood from invisible wounds. The broom writhed like a severed limb. Jamaaro dropped it in fear, and the old man rushed to pick it up. Before he could get it, Jamaaro overcame his fear and snatched it up again.

"Please," Oywetch said. "Give it back."

"Tell me about the song," Jamaaro said.

Oywetch dashed for the broom and Jamaaro jumped backwards. Oywetch missed, and went sprawling to the ground. He lay prostrate, breathing in the dust, looking at his bleeding palms. For a moment Jamaaro thought he would never get back up.

"Boket," Oywetch said. "He knows everything about her."

"Tell me!" Jamaaro hissed. The broom twisted and twirled, trying to break away from his hold, and his palm itched.

"I don't know," Oywetch said. "I heard a rumour that Boket knows. A rumour. They say she's not human and that she searches for laboki for unknown reasons but that's all I know."

Jamaaro vaguely knew about Boket, who he thought was a future kwaro. Jamaaro could not remember what kind of god he was destined to be, or what kind of stories he created, or even where he lived. He had first heard about him a long time ago, shortly after the success of Children of the Wound, and it had been a kind of urban legend that, now, he wondered if there was even a storyteller called Boket. They said he made an influential story that gave him a future kwaro status, but he served as laboki for only a few moons before his town replaced him because he was unable to create any more stories. Some said he had been cursed. Did that curse have something to do with Nyalisa? With the song?

"Where is this Boket?" he asked the old man.

"I don't know," Oywetch cried. "I only heard the rumour."

The broom was twisting and turning with increasing desperation, and Oywetch's hand now bled profusely.

"Please," he wept. "Give me the broom. I told you all I know."

Jamaaro wanted to interrogate him further, but did not think it was worth bothering over a wild rumour. He threw the broom at Oywetch and the old man scrambled for it like a cat jumping at a mouse. The moment Oywetch picked it up, his hand stopped bleeding.

"I'm sorry," Jamaaro said.

The old man gave him a scathing look, and then resumed sweeping, vigorously, throwing up such a huge dust cloud that it hid him.

Jamaaro walked back to the bruka, and soon he was pedalling hard. The ornithopter's wings flapped, slow, then fast, and faster, with big whooshing sounds. He pedalled harder and sweat broke out of his nape. The bruka's wings now beat a steady whoosh-whoosh rhythm. He released the jump-gear, and the bruka leaped into the air, jolting him. He pedalled harder, and in a few heartbeats he was soaring above his hut. Oywetch stood in the wang oo, the broom once again stuck to his hand, looking up at the bruka as if it were a strange kind of flying monster.

I came to find you. But why? She had said she needed his help because he was a future kwaro. Had she asked Boket for the same help before cursing him? But how, yet she was half his age, and, from what he remembered, Boket was more than three times his age. She was not yet born the time Boket made his story, so how could she have cursed him?

Could he trust anything Oywetch said?

She was human. She was afraid of her spirit dying, and he had looked into her eyes and seen that she had spoken the truth. She could not have been lying about that. She was human. A woman half his age. A beautiful woman. His goddess.

He wanted her to be human. He refused to believe she was some kind of creature.

Sweat drenched his cloth. Now that he was up in the air, he did not have to pedal hard. He engaged the coast-gear and the bruka glided over the town like a bird. He gave Wendo one last look, wondering if he would ever see it again. It was built with a fractal pattern that imitated a flower with twelve petals. The wang oo was at the centre, with the most influential homesteads bordering it. The streets of the town and the huts in each boma were arranged to imitate flowers, like a miniature version of the town, but the number of petals varied depending on the sise of the boma. The rwot's palace, the biggest of them all, had twenty five petals, and the smallest boma, like his, could not form petals because they had only one or two huts.

He flew away from the centre of the town, his bruka gliding just above the stone roofs, and then he was sailing over the gardens, over the grazing fields, and soon over the wilderness. A river cut through the land, a huge brown snake meandering through the vivid green, gashing through a narrow valley with a mighty roar, and then settling into a quiet, almost stationary, false lake that was a paradise of flowers. His favourite place.

He saw her at the shore. Her bark cloth, dyed a vivid red, stood out amid the dull grey rocks. She was not alone. There was someone with her. A man. Only one person in Wendo loved to dye his clothes to imitate a green leopard and he worked at the inn in which she had stayed. He called himself

Kwach but everyone called him Wodiel because he had the reputation of a horny goat. Even from all the way up here, he could hear her laugh and he knew she was very happy with him.

Happy with that piece of dung.

He choked. He did not want to land. He wanted to keep flying, to go far away from her.

He had imagined there was something special between them, the way she had looked into his eyes, the way a cloud of light had blossomed from her eyes and promised him the love he had been waiting for all his life, something had happened between them. Something special. Yet there she was, in a place that he had told her meant so much to him because he lay on those banks to daydream about stories. The place was his heart and she knew it. He had offered to pick her up from her inn to start their world tour, but she had said that she liked to walk at sunrise and she had asked if they could meet in this lake. "You make the flowers seem beautiful," she had said. "I'll walk over there and see them at sunrise. And it will be good luck to set off from a place that means so much to you." Her saying that could only mean there was something special between them. Yet there she was, holding hands with a dung of a man.

She is not human.

Was she yamo? Maybe those demons had figured out a way to get rid of their goatee. Was she planning to eat them both?

He wanted to ride away. He did not need her to see the world. He was better off alone, as he had always been. But pain flared in his chest and his eyes blurred with tears. She was his goddess, the one he had waited for all his life, so why was she at their meeting place with that piece of dung?

She saw him and she waved. They were standing too close to each other, holding hands.

He disengaged the glide-gear and tilted the fly-handle downwards, and the bruka dived toward the water. Too fast. It would be nice if he crashed into the river and smashed his head against rocks, that would be a merciful end to his pathetic life.

What good was he if he could not convince anyone to love him? Even after giving up his life to run away with her, even after promising to use all his powers to find her song, she chooses another man. A piece of dung. She sees that the future kwaro is hiding in the body of a dirty boy who lives with a drunkard father in a cave, and she prefers this dung to that boy.

Idiot.

He let go the fly-handle, and lost control of the ornithopter. It started to fall. He closed his eyes and lay back against the seat. The wind rushed in from the windows, making it hard for him to breath. The bruka spiralled. He wanted to sleep to stay calm. He feared panic would make him take control of the fly-handle again and he did not want that. This way was better. It beat another lifetime of loneliness.

He thought he could hear them scream. He thought it a good punishment for her to see him die.

The river rushed up at him. He closed his eyes tighter and then the crash came and all was black and silent.

Chapter Four

He saw lights, sparkling, blurry, encased in patches of green like a badly painted picture. It hurt him. He could not move, could not blink, could not close his eyes, could not wish the lights away. Was he in Pobur, the place everyone destined to be a god arrived at after death? He had only seen it in illustrations and none had depicted it as a badly painted image.

Why can't I move?

After a few more moments, his sight cleared a little and he became aware of yellow flowers clustered around his head. He loved their scent. They were familiar. Had he planted them? They sparkled when sunlight fell on their petals and they whispered sweet nonsense as the wind blew through them. He wanted to lie there and never wake up.

Am I dead?

Voices. A man and a woman. An argument. Maybe he was already hearing his first prayers as a kwaro of love. A couple was in trouble and he had to help them find… No. He knew the woman's voice. It had seduced him before, enchanted him. *It's not human.* Nyalisa? She sounded like a quacking duck, not like the beautiful olit bird. Maybe this is what she sounded like when she was angry. He could not make out what she was saying to the man. Wodiel. It sounded like a lover's quarrel.

Jamaaro listened carefully, filtering out the voices, and now he became aware of other sounds, crickets, a bumblebee, a frog, a pigeon. Now he knew why the yellow flowers seemed familiar. He was on the shore of the false lake at the river.

Am I still alive?

He could not feel his body. He tried to move, to feel pain, but he was hovering a few inches off the ground and the wind blew through him. He was dead but still trapped in his body – that worthless body. He would stay in this in-between state until an ajwaka freed him. That is what happened with suicides.

I threw it all away. A suicide kills the spirit. Once the ajwaka freed him, his spirit would wither into nothingness. He would never be a kwaro.

He had thrown it all away because he thought he was in love. *Thought.* He had met her just once, and he fell so madly that he committed suicide because she was with another man?

Something was not right… Had she enchanted him?

Women had rejected him before. Many, many times. She was not the first that he had imagined was his goddess. He had fallen madly in love before and they had all rejected him, yet he had never thought about killing himself. Why now?

Maybe kwaro would understand that he was not in control of his mind when he let go of the fly-handle. Maybe they would still make him a kwaro of love.

The voices got closer, and became more distinct. A lover's fight, indeed.

"You were stringing me along!" Wodiel shouted.

"Did I ever say I loved you?" Nyalisa said.

"But the way you looked into my eyes!" Wodiel said.

"Oh cheth!" Nyalisa said. "That's how I look at everybody!"

"Then why did you ask me to bring you here?" Wodiel said.

"I didn't ask!" Nyalisa said. "I wanted to walk and you insisted on flying me here and I accepted out of politeness. Did you take that to mean that I was in love with you?"

"You are mean!" Wodiel said. "You made me believe you loved me."

Jamaaro wanted to laugh. He now understood what kind of woman she was, and he felt so foolish for falling in love with her. She was just very friendly, overly friendly, so friendly that within moments of meeting anyone she talks to them as if she had known them all her life. Lonely men like him, and dung men like Wodiel who saw only sex in women, misread her.

Now he was dead. He had thrown his life away, his destiny as a god, all of it. He threw it away over a stupid suspicion. He got so angry with himself that he laughed in bitterness. Kwaro would never forgive him for this stupidity. He was not fit to be a god.

"Did he laugh?" Nyalisa said. She did not sound like a quacking duck, and her voice was once again as enchanting as that of a humming olit bird.

"Yes," Wodiel said, in a whisper of wonder. "How can he be alive?"

They heard me laugh?

Now the blurry green lights made sense, sunlight shining through leaves, a spectacle he enjoyed very much. He always dreamed of lying under a tree with his lover, watching the sun shine through the leaves. Though he had never gotten the chance to experience it, all his characters did, and it had become a favourite ritual for lovers. If they lay under a tree, holding hands in silence, and felt very happy watching the sunlight in the leaves, then they were truly in love.

A silhouette appeared, blocking the lights. Nyalisa. Though a shadow, he could see her large eyes, her high cheeks, the single strand of hair sticking out of her chin. He noticed that she had a perfectly heart-shaped cupid's bow, and it was a shade redder than the rest of her lips, which were a rich dark brown. He at first thought it was a spot of blood, then he thought it was a bit of dried make-up that she had forgotten to wash off, and then he wanted to take it as another sign that she was his goddess. He brushed the thought away. He had to stop thinking like that. She was not in love with him. She was just a friendly person.

"His eyes moved," she said.

*

He became aware of his body before he regained consciousness. He was dreaming, about a woman who had long dreadlocks that fell over her back, and there were beads of ice in the locks. The ice was not like the ice-pot pearls he had seen in the yamo dream. These ones looked like brightly coloured hailstones. Baraf, the woman called it. He knew it was honey-sweet without tasting it, because it was a dream. She plucked one off, put it in her palm and then used a thumb to grind it into a paste, which she smeared on his skin. Baraf materialised as if from secret pores in her hair, giving her an infinite supply. After a while, he noticed that the baraf had a coat of green cream, and his body was smeared in a sticky, green ointment. He wanted to stick out his tongue and taste it, but he knew it was not edible. It was medicine and it took away his pain.

His eyes opened. He could not see. No, he was not blind, he realised. Just in a dark place, a tiny dark place, in a cocoon made of leaves from the bondo tree. It had a strong smell, like stale fish. His body indeed was smeared in a green ointment, and he lay in a muddy puddle of it that had formed in the cocoon.

What did that dream mean?

He could move his hands. He was not bound, so he ruled out being kidnapped. Maybe he could rip his way out of the cocoon. He groped about in the darkness and touched the leafy wall, but it was too smooth, too slick, and he could not find any spot to grab and tear. He pushed hard against it and it bulged. It was elastic.

"He woke up," someone said. He knew that voice, someone he had once loved. Someone who never loved him back. "Let's get him out."

A zip whizzed, and then light hurt his eyes. He squinted, and sat up, and his pupils quickly adjusted to the brilliance. He saw her on a mat at the other end of the room, looking at him with large eyes, smiling without dimples, and yet still looking like a goddess of beauty. Nyalisa. He cursed. Why was she the first person he saw yet there were two other women in the room, sitting much closer to him? They had removed him from the cocoon.

He did not know the smaller of the two. She wore a yellow costume and he took her to be a healer's assistant. The other woman was Ayat, plump, chubby with deep dimples and with coloured shells decorating her dreadlocks. She was a future kwaro of healing and he thought he was in her healing house, which was more than a day's flight from Wendo. It made sense that he ended up at her place for no other musawo could rescue people from the in-between state.

"I greet you Jamaaro," Ayat said. "Good to see you after so long."

"I greet you Jamaaro," Nyalisa said. "I'm glad you woke up."

He touched his body, searching for bruises, for pain, but he could not feel anything, not even his own skin, for the ointment had become a second skin.

"You've been out for a whole moon and some days," Ayat said. "That medical skin has kept you alive and you'll live with it for another moon. It will peel itself off."

He had once loved her, desperately, and she had been in love with another man. He had created a story as a gift for her, and in the story she was the heroine. This made her one of only three people who had ever become his muse, and he thought her story was his best work. Its songs were the most popular, and favoured in all weddings, even though the lyrics bemoaned unreturned love. It would have been perfect, a kwaro of love and a kwaro of healing, they would have talked about them to the end of time.

"Do I have to stay here?" He croaked, his voice hurting with thirst.

"No," Ayat said. "From now on, that skin will work on you

on its own. I can ask Opili to fly you back home, but it will be better if you stayed here or somewhere close by so we can monitor your progress."

Unlike other healing houses, hers did not look plain and gloomy. The mats were vibrant with colour, the cushions looked like what you would find in a rwot's palace, and the walls were covered with beautiful murals. He gawped at them, for the murals were his drawings, and all were from her story. The theme image was a woman flying on the back of a red hen, a spear in hand, charging at a monster that had stolen her heart. Ayat had set up an image-wheel at one end of the room, one of the newer models that used the sun's light to run automatically, rather than the more popular model that relied on pedalling and so could be used anytime. A series of images ran on the wheel; the monster stealing her heart, the woman pursuing, stabbing it with her spear, and taking back her heart, in an endless loop.

"I can't stay," he said.

"I understand," Ayat said.

"I'll fly you back home," Nyalisa said.

"No!" he hissed.

"I brought you here," Nyalisa said. "I'll take you back."

He was quiet for a moment, still avoiding to look at her. You should have let me die, he wanted to say. It might not be a bad thing for his spirit to wither into nothingness. People did not love him. They loved *it*. They loved his work so much that they plastered images he had created all over their walls and they sang his songs at their weddings, but they did not love him. Why should he let them worship his spirit? Why should his spirit help them find happiness in love?

"Ask her to leave," he said to Ayat, in a soft voice.

A strangled sound emerged from Nyalisa, but he did not turn to see the look on her face, and she did not wait for Ayat to kick her out. He heard the mat rustle as she rose to her feet, and then almost noiselessly left the room. A heavy silence followed. Ayat's eyes burned into his flesh. He could feel her pity, and even before she spoke, her words hurt him deep.

"Did you do it because of her?"

He bit his lips hard. He did not think Nyalisa had told people what had happened, but that Wodiel, he must have told it with great relish. Now, maybe a storyteller somewhere was already creating a tale about a god of love who falls for a stranger, and kills himself when he finds her with another man. How would he live with that kind of shame?

"It was an accident," he said, aware that no one would believe him.

"I loved you," she said.

He looked up sharply. Her eyes were wet, and full of accusation. How could he attempt suicide over a woman he barely knew, and yet he did not do anything stupid when she had turned him down? Though they never became an item, they had connected in a deep way, which is why she cherished the story he made about her. He saw all this in her eyes and he felt sad.

"It was an accident," he said, and he hated the pathetic tone in his voice. He hated that his eyes became blurry, and he fought hard to keep the tears in check.

*

Ayat's healing house was built using a circle packing formula, just like her town used a circular fractal pattern. The huge huts were circles and each room was a perfect circle, creating circles inside of circles. As he walked out of the cocoon room, where they treated the critically ill, he realised his knees were so stiff that he limped. They would be stiff until the green skin peeled off. He walked into a very big circular room with beds arranged in rings, and it had twelve doors which led to cocoon rooms. The thirteenth door led to an even bigger room for the non-resident patients. It had cushioned mats on the floor, and eight doors. Seven doors led to wards like the one he had just passed and the eighth was the front door, large and circular, framing a courtyard in a bright and sunny day, birds making a racket in the shady trees, patients and their caretakers idling in the flowers, a solitary figure sitting under one tree. Nyalisa.

His chest tightened. The green skin suddenly felt too tight, and his knees felt stiff. He thought his vision was failing. He staggered out of the door, determined to keep walking straight to the gate and not to look at her. Yet something about the way she sat tugged at his heart. She leaned against the tree, her face turned upwards, her eyes closed, her hands clasped together on her laps, her legs spread out. She could have been meditating, but he could see tear tracks gleam with sorrow from deep inside.

Had his rejection hurt her this much? How could he walk away from that?

He stood there for a long time, watching her, and she seemed to have turned to stone. Then he found himself walking to her, and she seemed to sense his approach for she turned her face away, as if she did not want him to see the tear stains. Dead leaves crunched under his feet as he squatted beside her. She clamped her lips tight, and kept her face turned away. Fresh tears flowed out of her closed eyes.

I love you, he wanted to say. His heart was an over pressurised balloon, aching to tell her a lot of things. *I love you*. He wanted to scream at the top of his voice, scream until the whole world heard and the echoes boomed to the end of time. *I love you*. His throat ached, as if he had eaten too much salt. He knew he should apologise for asking Ayat to throw her out. He knew he should thank her for bringing him here and saving his life, for sitting faithfully by his side for a whole moon. He knew he should say things to take her hurt away, yet all he wanted was to tell her how much he loved her.

She buried her face in her palms and her body vibrated with soft sobs.

He sat down beside her. He wanted to hold her and make her happy. That is all that mattered to him, everything in the world revolved around that one thing. Her happiness. He wanted to brush away her tears and make her smile again.

"Come, fly me home," he said, his voice croaking. He sounded stupid, even to himself.

Coward! A voice yelled at him. Tell her what you really want to say!

"I enjoy your company," he said. "Very much," he added after a pause. "I was looking forward to our trip together."

Coward! The voice yelled. That's not what you want to say! Don't assume she knows. Tell her, tell her.

Her sobs hit a higher note. She seemed to have sunk deeper into pain.

"Go away," she cried. "Please just go away."

He stood up, aware that he had yet again bungled an opportunity to find love. He should have accepted her offer to fly him back home. Now, whatever he said sounded false. He walked away, thinking he would never see her again.

Chapter Five

He could not get her off his mind. He hated himself for dreaming about her every night, for thinking about her every moment of the day. She filled his head with images of a woman with ice pearls dangling on her beard, and he wanted to rip his head off to get her out.

His first impulse had been to investigate Oywetch's rumour, and he had hit an immediate dead end. The wang oo keeper in Ayat's town said there once had been a storyteller called Boket, who became a future kwaro of peace after his story put an end to war. Strangely, he failed to create any other story, and his town replaced him after a few moons. He lived a long time ago, way before Jamaaro's grandfather was born. He could not still be alive. Whatever rumour Oywetch had heard was so distorted that it did not have any truth.

Jamaaro found a place to stay, about half a day's walk from Ayat's town, but in a bruka it took about the time a family needed to eat a meal, so he could quickly get help in case of an emergency. The town, Kapendo, died on failing to keep a good laboki. Weeds strangled the streets and hordes of lizards lived in the abandoned homesteads. Other than a few chicken and ducks, no bird had visited in a very long time. Only about five hundred people remained, and they flew to Ayat's town to consume stories to sustain what was left of their miserable lives.

He could hide here until he recovered, since the town got no regular visitors. The green skin covered every inch of his body, hiding his identity. He told the town folk that he hated the depressing atmosphere of a healing house but, his home being a whole moon's flight away, he needed to stay close to Ayat until he recovered. Desperate for new neighbours, they accepted his tale without questions. Maybe this was kwaro's doing to revive their town.

Ayat gave him medicine to help cultivate a new look. By the time the green skin peeled off, he would have grown a large beard, bushy eyebrows, and thick dreadlocks. Then, he hoped to spend the rest of his life roaming the world, disguised as an anonymous and freelancing storyteller, never to be a laboki again.

"Yours is a lonely fate," Ayat told him. "To be a kwaro of love, your heart must be free for everyone. You can't lock it up by loving only one person. You'll be alone in this life, and you'll be even lonelier in the next for you'll be scattered in many thousands of shrines, with thousands of hands seeking your blessing at the same moment, and it will be just as if it is wind fondling you. They'll worship you, but they won't really love you. They'll ask for blessings, but won't give you anything in return. That's your fate. You'll give love, but never receive it."

He did not want to be a kwaro anymore. He wanted the warmth of a woman in his bed, to know what it felt like for another person to love him. Ayat had told him what he had known all along, what he feared to even think about, that he was destined to grow old alone. Gods were lonely people, after all. He hated kwaro for choosing him, and he hated them even more for giving him a heart that fell in love at the slightest provocation, that fell so madly in love yet the woman would never love him back. If they wanted him to grow old alone, they should have made him immune to the stupidity of his heart. But here he was, yet again miserable, with yet another woman in his head, haunting him with her beautiful eyes, torturing him with her sweet voice, giving him nightmares with her iced beard. Here he was, loving her desperately, yet cursed never to receive her love.

How could he live with such pain?

She was lodged in his head. He thought she lived just behind his eyes, and he could hear the squishing as she walked through his brain, the scratching as she scraped his skull for food, the gurgling as she sucked blood out of his veins. She was there, a parasite.

How could he live with that agony?

He wanted to jump into a bruka and crash in a desolate place where no one would find his body. Then, maybe then, he would find peace. True peace. He would not become a kwaro and he would not be scattered in thousands of shrines all over the world to suffer an eternity of loneliness just so other people could be happy. He would find joy in the nothingness.

The green skin made his knees very stiff; he could not fly a bruka. He had to wait to kill himself. He had to endure another moon of agony with her in his head. He could not bear that, not even another day of this torture.

He knew only one way to heal. Creating stories. If she became a figment of his imagination then, whenever she cropped up he would daydream about the story. Not her. With time, she would be relegated to that harmless place where his characters lived in a happy little town of their own. He would find peace.

Maybe. Just maybe.

He began to draw her as he saw her in his dreams, and to create a story about a woman with a long strand of hair curling out of her chin. She grows baraf on this beard, sweet honey and cream ice, which she uses to lure children into her home. She eats the children, for she is a kind of yamo that does not have the tell-tale goatee. One day, she finds a man with a sweet tooth and he hungers for her baraf. She thinks it a nice change of diet to eat an adult, and so she lures him into her hut. However, he is a storyteller and he has a magic adungu that he inherited from his mother. It stirs love in the hearts of whoever listens to it. After he has had his fill of baraf, he strums the harp and sings of her beauty. The song enchants her, and she wants to hear him sing every night before she sleeps and every morning when she wakes up. She can't eat him. They get married. She stops eating people because she wants to be a normal wife. But her appetite for flesh is so strong. The more she loves him, the more the demon in her thinks of him as the most delicious meal she has ever had. So, one morning while he sleeps, she sneaks out of their bed and he never sees her again.

The man grows sad. He searches for her all over in vain. He writes a song about the lover who vanishes from his bed and wanders the world, singing, searching, begging her to return. Wherever he goes, people tell him he has never married, that he doesn't have a wife. Finally, he visits an ajwaka for a divination, and learns that he married a strange kind of yamo that does not grow a goatee. It didn't eat him because it fell in love with him. The storyteller, in a bottomless pit of sadness, asks the ajwaka for magic shoes to take him to Wori, the underworld village of yamo. He wants to find her. The ajwaka tells him other yamo will eat him but he can't live without her. So, he wears the magic shoes and they take him to Wori. He plays his adungu and sings the song he wrote for her as he enters this dark, dark world. Yamo come out in hordes to eat him, but when they hear his harp, it stirs love in their hearts, and they can't eat him. Still, he cannot find his wife because, in Wori, yamo do not look like women and they do not remember their life as humans. He settles in Wori, teaching yamo music, hoping that one day his wife will reveal herself. In the end, yamo become good musicians and music transforms their dark village into a colourful and magical land. They stop eating people, and instead they take on a new profession, being a muse to musicians.

A happy ending. A good love story.

Jamaaro drew the images with a feverish desperation. He churned out more than thirty every day and when he played them on the image-wheel they span at a pace of twelve images per heartbeat, creating the illusion of motion. In the mornings he wrote down the rhymes and prose for the oral narration and, in the afternoon, he drew, and he kept drawing late into the night. Days passed in a daze, and nights sailed by like thick clouds. He left the easel only to get food from his doorsteps. He paid a little boy to bring him the food, which the boy's mother cooked. He went to the door only when he was hungry, and the food would be long cold. For long stretches of time, he would not know if it was day or night. He would fall asleep on his easel and when he awoke, he would right away pick up where he had dozed off.

He liked the story very much, aware that for the first time he was creating one that did not have any fantastical creatures, one firmly grounded in reality. A simple love story with everyday creatures like husbands and wives and yamo. There was the wishful thinking of turning a race of demons into beings that fed on music rather than on people, but that was the only fantastical thing and it was not a farfetched imagination. He felt the story would be his best, that it would be retold a billion times by a billion other storytellers.

But he needed a song to complete it.

A complex song to suit every mood in every chapter. Some stanzas would be fast and furious and upbeat to make people dance, others would be slow and sweet to make people cry in happiness. Some would be off-key and discordant to create a sense of horror, and yet others would be cheesy enough to make people laugh. The chorus had to have easy lyrics and a simple beat for everyone in the wang oo to join in, clapping in rhythm with the drums and stamping their feet along with the dancers. The chorus would serve as interludes, and transitions from the parts that would be told with images to parts that would need actors and to parts that would have only dancers and musicians.

Since he thought her voice was like that of the humming olit bird, he used the bird's tune for an inspiration. He needed musical instruments to compose the song, and he knew he was taking a risk when he asked his errand boy for help. The ghost town would now know he was a storyteller, but he hoped they would not figure out his true identity. He hoped that at worst they would ask him to be their laboki, and he might create for them just one story as gratitude for their hospitality. The boy easily procured everything he needed. After the death of the town's last laboki, there had been no one to use her story creation tools.

He strummed the adungu, blew the horn, played the drums, and beat by beat, the song came to life in his tunemaker.

One night, as he was lost in the rhythm, it struck him that his lyrics were eerily similar to those of the song Nyalisa wanted to find. Was it because they had the same theme, of a man searching for his wife?

He begun to think that maybe she was not looking for a song. Maybe she had planted the idea of the song in him so he could make it for her.

Many people offered him wealth to be characters in his stories, but he never accepted. Only thrice had he written stories based on actual people, his elder brother, Akela, and Ayat, people who had stirred his life so much that he immortalised them in his creations. Maybe Nyalisa had enchanted him so he could immortalise her in a story.

I don't want my spirit to die.

His elder brother, whose spirit faded away into nothingness after his suicide, in a way remained alive in Jamaaro's breakout story. Every time Children of the Wound was retold, his brother's heart beat again, and since the story was so influential it was remixed and repackaged in a thousand different ways, and each time it was told, his brother came to life. Maybe Nyalisa hoped for this kind of eternal life.

He hated himself for falling into her trap.

He wanted to stop creating her story, but the alternative was the agony of thinking about her as a real person. He wished the green skin could already peel off so that he could go somewhere and dash a bruka against a cliff.

And yet, now that the story had taken hold in his mind, he knew that he would not kill himself before finishing it, and it would take him several moons to complete. Maybe ten, maybe twenty. That is what had kept him alive all along, the compulsion to finish a story. And once it was done, there another would already be ringing in his head, begging him to create it.

He laughed at himself. At the fake lake, the heat of the moment had enabled him to let go the fly-handle, but such a moment would never come again. He was stuck in this world.

The days passed and Ayat's camouflage medicine took effect. His beard grew big, his eyebrows became bushy, and dreadlocks snaked out of his head like enchanted ropes. The story matured, and the song took a life of its own. He worked with ever increasing desperation, for he did not want to spend too long in that dead town. He could not create the story while on the road for he could not carry all the musical instruments with him. He had to finish it before he left, and once on the road, he would not create such lengthy epics.

One morning, when the new moon appeared like a thin banana, a knock on the door interrupted his frustrations. For a moment he thought it was the boy who ran his errands, yet he frowned for the boy had made a delivery a short while ago, and he always shouted out a friendly 'vipi' in greeting.

The knock persisted, and so, grumbling, he went to the door.

The hut he lived in once belong to a large family, probably the patriarch's for it was in the centre of a boma with a triangular fractal pattern. When he opened the door, he saw huts tapering off toward a magnificent gate, all empty and overgrown with weeds. The pathways, once paved with blue stones, were buried under a tumble of grass.

At first, he saw no body, and he cursed, thinking some child was playing a prank on him. Then an old man, who must have become impatient when he did not answer immediately and had been trying to peep in through a window, walked into his view, from the back of the hut. His name was Rakome and he had a broom stuck in his hand. The town's wang oo keeper. Though not in use, they maintained a wang oo hoping a miracle would make it useful again. Dirt had filled in his wrinkles; he wore dirty rags and weeds grew out of his greyed hair. The broom, mouldy and smothered in cobwebs, looked like it would fall apart if he started sweeping. If the town recovered, he would regenerate into an ordinary old person. If the last family left the town and it died, he would turn into a tree in the wang oo.

"I greet you Jamaaro," Rakome said.

Jamaaro felt a flash of panic at the mention of his name. He should not have asked for those musical instruments. But, he thought, if the whole town knew, the rwot would have come knocking, not this cleaner.

"I don't know that name," he said, and made to close the door, but the old man grabbed it and with a supernatural strength, preventing him from closing it.

"You can't fool these old eyes," Rakome said.

"Please go away," Jamaaro said. "I won't be your laboki."

"I wish I could ask you to," Rakome said. "You could save our town, but we will wait for another opportunity from kwaro. Greater powers have called you."

"Greater powers?" Jamaaro asked.

"Boket wants to see you," Rakome said.

"Boket?" Jamaaro said. "That kwaro of peace?"

"He never became kwaro."

"He can't possibly be still alive."

"He's sending someone for you."

Jamaaro clenched the paint brush so tight that it broke. If Boket, a man who was telling stories before Jamaaro's grandfather was born, was still alive, then he was not human. Maybe there was truth in the rumour.

"What do you mean greater powers?" Jamaaro said.

"I can't say," Rakome said. "I just know they are not to be disobeyed. They warned me not to tell my town about you and it hurts me that –"

"I can't refuse?" Jamaaro said, interrupting.

The old man shook his head. "He says you should give him one drawing of Nyalisa that you have made."

Jamaaro swallowed hard. He wanted to ask many questions, but the stone in his throat was so big that he could not speak.

Chapter Six

The flight to Dokelo town took four days. It sat at on a plateau on the side of a small mountain and from a distance it looked like a collection of nests. It had a complex fractal design with bird motifs. Every boma had a fence that looked like something a bird had built. The huts were not cylindrical with cone-shaped roofs, like in other towns, but were metallic eggs. The shiny walls caught the reflection of the sky and the surroundings, giving them an illusion of paintings. It was a very prosperous town of nearly fifty thousand people, and its wang oo was a pit with stepped sides on which thirty thousand people could sit comfortably. The wang oo's keeper, a little overweight and with a protuberant belly, looked a lot younger than his age and he wore fine cotton clothing and his broom had a gold-coated handle. His teeth were made of gold. Even his shoes spoke of wealth for they were made of crocodile skin bedecked with shells.

"I greet you Jamaaro," the keeper said, as the bruka pilot helped Jamaaro climb off the ornithopter. They had landed in the keeper's boma which, being the home of a spirit, was in the middle of a banana plantation. "Welcome to Dokelo town."

"Eh yii," Jamaaro said.

"Can I see?" the keeper said.

Jamaaro gave him a piece of bark cloth with a drawing and the keeper unfurled it with great relish, as though it were a precious gift. A big smile erupted on his face as he ogled at the coloured sweet ice on Nyalisa's strange beard.

"Wow," the keeper said. "Such a wonderful depiction of her." He started to walk away, without waiting for a response, still admiring the drawing.

Jamaaro was even more confused since the pilot had not told him anything during the flight. He could not walk much because of the green skin, so the pilot put him in a wheelchair, and he rolled after the keeper. They went to a boma quite a walk away, and throughout the keeper ogled at the drawing, chuckling to himself, ignoring Jamaaro. The fence of this boma looked like a hammerkop's nest, and the gate was the sculpture of that bird's head. They walked in through the mouth, and the driveway, the tongue, had soft red sand. From ground level view, the egg-shaped huts were even more gigantic, and Jamaaro could not imagine why they needed such big homes. The walls were like a mirror, and he wondered where they got all that metal to build an entire town.

They went into the centre most hut and the moment they entered the keeper closed the door, plunging them in pitch darkness. However, in the brief moment of light, Jamaaro had noticed the room was so large that twenty people could have comfortably had a dance fest in it. The walls were covered with drawings, and something crouched in the middle; he could not be sure what creature it was.

"I greet you Jamaaro," the crouching thing spoke, in the husky voice of an old man.

"Eh yii," Jamaaro replied, hesitant.

"The light hurts me," the creature said again. "You need star-glasses."

The keeper, who did not need the special glass to see in the darkness, put something in Jamaaro's hands. They felt like a pair of shells on a string. Jamaaro put one over each eye and tied the string at the back of his head. After a moment, he could see in the darkness, though everything had a bluish haze. The creature looked like a very old person with a face so wrinkled that Jamaaro could not tell the eyes from the mouth. It sat with the chin resting on the knees, arms wrapped around the legs, and it shivered as though it had the chills of malaria.

"Boket?" he said.

"Eh yii," the creature said. "I'm Boket, once a future kwaro of peace, now the ghost that blesses this town with wealth and power."

Jamaaro had never experienced the story that Boket created. People said it was meant for times of war and they had known peace for so long that war had become a myth. At the time it was made, a great war burned the entire world and it reimagined histories such that people stopped seeing themselves as enemies. They embraced each other as siblings with different mothers.

The room was bare, with not even a mat on the floor, except for the drawings that were pinned on every inch of the wall. For a moment, Jamaaro was confused. They seemed to be from the same story, for they all depicted different kinds of creatures with a particular face.

Nyalisa's face.

His heart beat erratically, like hailstones hammering an iron sheet. He got off the wheelchair and hobbled closer to the drawings. They were indeed of Nyalisa, each a different version of her. Hundreds upon hundreds of them. His head was in a whirlwind. His vision became blurry. He could no longer feel the ground under his feat. The room spun in a terrible maelstrom. He retched. He clamped his mouth shut, afraid puke would spill on the images, *on her*. He could not take his eyes off them, *off her*, he could not step away from them. From her! His skin was on fire. The green skin was alive and squeezing life out of him.

"You see why I called you?" Boket said.

They were not from a single creator. They were from many, many creators, and each had drawn their fantasy of her, with the only constant being her face. This one saw her as a horned flying lizard, that one thought she was an elephantine thing, the other one imaged her as some sort of eagle, while this one dreamed of her as a humanoid fish-thing. Jamaaro thought his fantasy of her, with pearls of sweet ice on a beard, was tamely realistic, and yet he was supposed to be one of the most fantastical creators.

They all drew her at the same age, and yet, telling from the paint, the bark cloth, and the drawing techniques, some images were very old. Some were several generations older than Boket, who had lived before Jamaaro's grandfather was born. Still, they all gave her the face of a girl transforming into a woman, just past the age at which she is allowed to marry.

"We all fell in love with her," Boket said.

Jamaaro found the image of Nyalisa that Boket had drawn,

encased in a gold frame with a caption saying it was the theme picture from the peacebuilding story. She was an eagle-like woman armed with a shield and an arrow-gun, but instead of arrow-missiles flowers peeped out of the quiver on her back. Jamaaro had seen versions of this drawing, but now looking at the original, he thought the reproductions did not capture the essence of the princess who convinced the world to discard arrows and embrace flowers. None had even come close to drawing her in the likeliness of Nyalisa.

"She filled me with dreams," Boket said. "She gave me such beautiful dreams and I had to tell her story." He was quiet for a moment, as if talking cost him a lot of energy and he had to catch his breath. "I was young then, struggling to make my name. Then I met her, and I fell madly in love. She became my muse. She told me about the song, and she asked me to help her find it. The idea of wandering the world with her by my side was a sweet dream, but I already had a tune for her lyrics, and a story to go with it. I didn't need to go around the world with her. I knew I had found the muse who would make me a great, great laboki."

Jamaaro felt a hot stone in his chest. He felt used, like ash that the cook throws away. *She is not my goddess.* The realization strangled him. Every one of these creators, and there were hundreds, maybe thousands more whose drawings had not ended up in the hut, they had all thought she was their goddess. He had suspected it at the riverside when he saw her with Wodiel, that she was just an overly friendly person, but when he had started to create her story he had imagined that maybe there was something special between them after all, for he could not feel so strongly about someone who did not feel the same way about him. Now seeing thousands of other storytellers had thought the same left a bitterness in his mouth. She was just using him.

"When you finish her story," Boket said, "it's the last one you'll ever tell."

His voice had gotten lower, and the words come out with great difficulty, one at a time, as if he was pulling a huge stone up a steep hill. But when Jamaaro turned to him, he saw that Boket held his version of Nyalisa in his hands, and it was giving him an orgasm.

"She eats our imagination," Boket said.

A long red thing covered in goo, that Jamaaro thought was a tongue, stuck out of a hole in what he thought was the creature's face, and it was licking the drawing, licking the sweet coloured ice that dangled on her beard.

She's a yamo, Jamaaro thought. A strange kind of yamo. She did not feast on flesh but on the spirit. Now, he understood the dream that came the night he met her, and he understood why he had written a story about a yamo that did not have a goatee. Kwaro was telling him about her, warning him. Was that story also a prophecy? He thought about the last time they had met, how she had told him to 'go away.' Surely, at that time he was already in her trap, so why did she let him go? Had she spared him because she had, truly, fallen in love with him?

"She prefers struggling storytellers who she can manipulate into thinking she is a muse." Boket continued, saliva drooling out of the mouth-hole. "But she's really the anti-muse."

The keeper snatched the drawing from Boket.

"You'll ruin it!" the keeper hissed.

He used a handkerchief to wipe the drool off the bark cloth, and then he used his broom to sweep at the drawing, as if it had dirt, and pearls of coloured sweet ice fell to the floor. Boket's tongue darted out like that of a lizard aiming for a fly and gobbled up the ice. He let it fill his mouth, and he went into a swoon.

"I taste her lips," Boket whispered. "Only a genius can put accurate taste in an image."

Boket's face turned up towards the keeper, like a dog begging for more treats, but the keeper was frowning at Jamaaro. He looked at the image as if inspecting it for new clues, and then used his broom to sweep it again. Pearls of ice tinkled on the floor. Boket's tongue flicked out and gobbled them up, one at a time, making each last as long as possible.

The keeper picked one pearl, and held it close to his eyes, as though surprised at his own magic. He tasted the ice, then put it on his tongue and it dissolved into a rainbow paste. He swallowed, and the frown gave way to an expression of pure pleasure.

Jamaaro could not understand what they thought they were tasting, for he had never kissed Nyalisa, how then could he put the taste of her lips in the drawing?

Boket again looked up at the keeper, begging for more ice, and when the keeper started to roll up the drawing, Boket's body sagged in disappointment.

"Creating her story opened a door in my mind, for her to enter," Boket said, the panting now clear in his voice. "Making love to her, kissing her, oh my," he paused, relishing the memories, "it gave her a bed in my soul, just as if I'd married her. By the time I finished the story she was a part of me and nothing I did could get rid of her. Oh no, I didn't want to get rid of her. I enjoyed every moment. She slowly ate my imagination. Oh, the sweetest feeling. It gave me an infinite orgasm. I begged her to eat it all up at once, but she took her time, nibbling, nibbling, nibbling, in an infinity of lovemaking, and I didn't want it to end."

He fell quiet for a moment, and when he resumed talking, his voice was raspy for the sweet memories had come to an end.

"She left. After she had eaten up my imagination, she left." His voice was wheezy, as though he was struggling to breathe. "You see, imagination is the essence of the spirit, so when she ate my gift, she beheaded my spirit and I could not become kwaro. I got stuck here. I can't die. I can't live. I can't create. The only thing I think of is her. My Nyalisa."

Jamaaro turned away from the creature and again stared at the drawings, wondering which was a worse fate, suffering an eternity of loneliness as a kwaro of love, or turning into a creature stuck somewhere worse than the in-between place, loving a woman who was only using him, and unable to let go. What a sad life, he thought. He wondered if other creators had the same story, of broken hearts, of unreturned love, of being unable to let go and turning into things that sat in the dark, forever aching for her.

"We think only future kwaro become a blessing," the keeper said.

Jamaaro turned to him, for a moment he could not understand what the keeper was talking about, and then he remembered how Boket had introduced himself, *the ghost that blesses this town with wealth and power.*

"We believe you too will bring us great blessings." He was smiling, his gold teeth seemed to shine. "We'll give you anything you want," the keeper continued. "You see?" His broom swept around the room, showing off the drawings. "Boket wants these, so our people search the world to find them. Whenever we hear of a struggling storyteller, we send scouts to see if she'll come calling, and we do all this to keep Boket happy. Whatever you want, we'll give you."

"Me?" Jamaaro said, not sure what else to say.

"Yes," the keeper said. "We could even make another woman to look like her so you can be with her for eternity. I hear you never married. I hear you never found love. I hear you tried to kill yourself because she was with another man." The keeper was grinning, his gold teeth appeared to be on fire. "I'll make all that go away. I'll give you the love that has eluded you all your life."

"No," Jamaaro hissed.

"You can't escape her," the keeper said. "She's in your head and you are creating her story. You can't escape. She'll eat your gift. She'll eat your imagination and behead your spirit and you'll end up like that." He used his broom to point at Boket, and for a moment Jamaaro saw himself growing impossibly old in a bare room, turning into something quite not human, torturing himself with images of a lover he could never have. "Whatever you want, you'll get."

"No," was all Jamaaro could say.

"We've adopted you," the keeper said. "We'll help you to finish her story."

"You –" Jamaaro tried to protest, to say he did not want to finish the story, not anymore, but the words dried up when he realised that they had kidnapped him. They wouldn't let him go. They wanted Nyalisa to eat his imagination, and then they would use him as a charm to bless their town.

"Finish her story," the keeper said again, still grinning.

Chapter Seven

They put him in a hut in the same boma with Boket, and he learned that the boma was a prison for her victims. They had kidnapped over a hundred other storytellers, for the town's scouts were constantly searching for her victims. Whenever they heard of a struggling storyteller, they sent spies, knowing she would come knocking. They wanted another charm to bless their town, for as Boket aged, his charm waned. They did not know exactly why he had become a blessing, and they were experimenting with Jamaaro being a future kwaro status. If he failed, they would bury him alive and he would suffer an eternity in a coffin, yearning for a love he could never have, torturing himself with memories of her.

His hut was thrice larger than the one in Wendo. It had a spring bed with a soft mattress and a warm fur blanket, an ice pot that made sweet and creamy baraf, which he never touched, and a creation table where he set up his easel. A set of musical instruments were stacked on one side, while an image-wheel was on one wall. It ran on the sun's light during the day and on a wind pedal during the night, which made watching images on it frustrating. They had brought everything he had made on the story while in Kapendo, the drawings, the rhyme and prose. They had even brought for him the creation box where he kept the five unfinished works and the tune-maker in which he had stored fragments of songs, and fragments of *her* song, but he did not have the energy to continue the story.

Was it prophetic? Why else had he imagined her as a yamo without a goatee?

The long trip to Dokelo had left him physically exhausted and learning about Nyalisa had drained all his mental strength. For several days and nights, he lay inert in bed, unable to sleep, unable to eat, staring blankly at the domed ceiling, and he resolved to stop making her story. It was the only way to beat her. Dokelo town might keep him prisoner, but they could not force him to finish the story. He had reluctantly succumbed to creating it, hoping to heal, but now he had a very strong motivation to stop.

You can't escape her, the keeper had said.

Boket had also said that love making was essential for her to access and eat a storyteller's imagination. Jamaaro had a chance for he had not even kissed her. He just had to stop creating the story, to destroy whatever he had made for it, the drawings, the music, the rhymes and the prose, and he would survive.

But he could not bring himself to do it. The story was his child. No parent could kill his own child…. He had to fight with himself to destroy it, and he would have to fight an even bigger battle to avoid recreating it, for destroying would not erase them off from his head.

After a few days of not eating, he was dizzy with hunger, and for a moment he contemplated starving to death, but that would be a suicide and he would be stuck in the in-between place. Dokelo might not allow an ajwaka to free him from his body. They might bury him in that state, and he would suffer the same, just as if she had eaten his imagination.

Burn it!

He started to eat. The servant who brought the food lit up in excitement, and Jamaaro heard him run away, calling the keeper, who came shortly after and had a big smile on seeing that Jamaaro had indeed ended the hunger strike.

"It's hard to accept such a fate," the keeper said. "But it's your future. We shall do everything we can to make you happy."

Jamaaro had not bothered to remember the keeper's name, nor that of any of the servants, nor that of the rwot, who never left his palace because he was so fat that he could not pass through doors. The keeper ran the town.

"Let me go," Jamaaro said. "She won't eat my mind."

"Don't fool yourself," the keeper said.

"I never made love to her," Jamaaro said. "So even if I finish the story, she won't eat my imagination and you won't get your good luck charm. Let me go."

The keeper looked at him for a long time, and then chuckled in derision. "You are a bad liar," the keeper said.

"It's the truth," Jamaaro said.

"You think we'll let you go on such a lie?" the keeper said. "No man can resist such a beautiful woman, especially not you who is so desperate for love. Finish the story."

The days passed and the green skin peeled off his body. He took a bath, finally, and could once again feel his skin. He had control of all his joints again, so he started to think about escape.

They treated him more like a guest than a prisoner, and they allowed him to walk around town, though two armed guards followed him wherever he went and locked him in at night. The only feasible way out of the town was on a bruka, for the steep mountain made for arduous climbing. There was no bruka in the boma they kept him in, but every other boma in the neighbourhood had one, and they did not have gates for they were ordinary homesteads. His biggest obstacle, he saw, would be the guards who kept a keen watch.

He could not devise a plan to beat them for she was a constant in his head. The tune he had made for her echoed in his head like a mad bat shrieking in a cave. He daydreamed about the story until his head ached, as if his brain had separated from his skull and was sloshing about like porridge in a calabash. He wanted to cry.

A large part of story creation happened when he was daydreaming. As he lay on the bed, as he walked about the town, as he ate food, as he experienced a story in the wang oo, he could not stop it. He tried hard not to work on her story, but he could not stop from drifting into reveries about it, and then the urge to draw a scene, or improve the song, would overwhelm him.

"I heard you create stories faster than this," the keeper told him one day.

"Let me go," Jamaaro said. "She won't eat my mind."

"Finish the story quickly," the keeper said.

"Why the rush?" Jamaaro said.

"It's a good story," the keeper said. "I want to know how it ends."

Jamaaro, too, wanted to know the ending. The plot outline was in his head, and like always he resisted writing it down for that would be like writing it on stone. He wanted the freedom to make changes, for new ideas to surprise him. Would the protagonist charm yamo into being good creatures or would they eat him? Would he find his wife, or would the current ending stay? He wanted to know, and he feared he would never really abandon the story.

But, if he started to obsess over another story, he would gradually forget hers. It would take time, maybe many moons, maybe longer, but he would forget.

Would he?

Burn it!

He would not move on if its products were lying about. Each time he saw the drawings, it worsened his obsession. Whenever he read the rhymes and prose, and when he played back extracts of the song, it fuelled his daydreams. He had to burn it, all of it, and that would be the first step to getting her out of his head.

What if she truly loves me?

He waited for the middle of the night. The servants had locked him in and retreated to their own hut. He took out all the drawings, all the notes, the rhymes and the prose, and he piled them up on the floor. He opened his tune-maker and ripped off strips of tape in which he had stored the song, and added them onto the pile.

He sat on the bed, staring at the heap for a long moment, at his *child*, looking for strength from deep inside to burn it. He closed his eyes and pictured Boket, and then he found courage to light a match. He opened his eyes and saw the match burning on a piece of bark cloth. For a moment he feared the back cloth would not catch fire, and then it burst into flame and the flame spread quickly. The hut became warmer.

Being on a mountain, the town was very cold. After the green skin had peeled off, he had taken to wearing layers of warm clothing, even when going to sleep. The hut was designed to trap the sun's heat and kept warm through the night, and now the fire added to that warmth, and sweat ran down his cheeks.

He trembled in pain, watching his child die. He wanted to beat the flames out with the blanket. He wanted to empty the contents of the ice pot onto the flames. He bit his lips and clenched his fist and fought hard with himself.

Thick smoke covered the room and choked him. He staggered to the window and threw it open. A cold blast of air hit him. He welcomed the distraction. He stayed at the window, his face freezing and smoke swirling around him, until the flames fizzled out.

Then he closed the window, entered the bed, and blew out the tadooba, but he could not stop shivering. He dressed up in a sheep wool robe and pulled the blanket over his head, and it helped a little bit, but the cold still gnawed at his bones. An eternity passed. He cried for morning, when the sun would rise and the hut would gobble up its light to warm him, but time stood still, and the cold was relentless.

Then, he heard the door opening and he jerked to a sitting position.

Had the smoke attracted the guards? It did not matter. He had already destroyed the story. He pulled the blanket tighter around him, a sheet of ice still on his face, and waited as the locks clicked and clacked. The door swung open, and a shadow stood in the moonlight. Though a feather blanket disguised her form, he knew who it was. He could feel her presence in his head.

"Nyalisa," he said, aware that he was saying her name aloud for the first time.

"I looked everywhere for you," she said. "Can I come in?"

For a moment, he regretted burning the story. If he had procrastinated just a little longer, she would have found it intact. She would have seen his rendition of her, and she would –

It's a trap, a voice yelled at him.

Making love to her, Boket had said, *gave her a bed in my soul, just as if I'd married her.*

That's why she had come, he thought. To seduce him.

"It's cold," she said. "Can I come in?"

Yes, he almost said, but he thought it was a trick question. She might be asking to come into his life, not into the hut, and if he said yes, she would never leave.

After a long moment when he did not respond, she closed the door, plunging the room into pitch darkness. The tadooba and box of matches sat on a stool beside the bed. He scratched a match, on the wall and it flared, throwing a dull light on her. She had a new hairstyle, plaited in little heaps like a potato garden, and she was wrapped up in a thick feather blanket. She was smiling at him.

He did not see a mind-eating yamo. He saw a beautiful young woman with enchanting eyes and with a bewitching smile. His goddess.

"I love you," she whispered.

She took several steps toward the bed, hesitant, and now she stood about a pace away from the pile of ash, which she seemed not to have noticed. She looked at him and he knew he had to say something in response, but his mind was blank.

"I know they've told you things about me," she said. "I can understand if you never want to see me again, for it is true, everything they said. I'm that monster."

She was quiet for a moment, pausing for effect. He knew for if he were making such a story, he would have made her pause after making such a huge confession, and just before she said the next important thing.

"You have to know that I fell truly in love with you," she said, and he thought, *just like in the story*. "That's why I never did anything bad to you. I love you and I need you in my life. You can change me. You are a future kwaro of love and you can put love in my heart. You can destroy the demon in me and turn me into a good person."

Just like in the story.

The match burned down, and the flame touched his skin. He threw it away with an "Ouch!", but quickly struck another, afraid that one more moment of darkness and she would disappear. He lit the lamp, and it threw a red glow on her.

I love you too, he nearly said. He swallowed hard, something choking him.

Had she enchanted him into thinking that the story was prophetic? Had she put the story in his head?

Finally, she noticed the ash, and frowned. She picked up something, a scrap of unburnt bark cloth, part of an image that had survived, her face still on it.

"Aww," she said, and he did not know if it was pleasure on discovering he had drawn her, or pain that he had burned up the story.

"I heard you were writing about me," she said, not taking her eyes off the fragment, fire dancing in her pupils. "So, I came to see."

The keeper must have put word out to lure her to his town. He had probably decided that if Jamaaro was lying, she would not respond, but if he had never made love to her, she would be looking for him. He must have gladly given her the key to his hut the moment she showed up.

"Did you burn it?" she said.

He was destined to be a kwaro of love, he thought. He was not supposed to fall in love, so kwaro could not have made him fall for this demon.

He needed a weapon.

The only thing within reach was his motion brush, with which he sketched the edges of characters such that when played on the image-wheel they seemed to move fast. It was about half the length of his arm and, unlike a bristled brush that used paint, it had a sharpened tip through which ink flowed onto the paper. It could stab.

"I'll draw it again," he said, his voice strangely calmer than he felt.

He slid off the bed and walked toward the easel, which was further inside the room, away from her. The brush sat in a tin attached to the easel stand. He took it, feeling the coldness of its metal, and then turned to face her.

She had squatted, and was sorting through the ash, finding pieces of drawings and bits of texts. She found a singed strip of tape and tears ran down her face.

"My song?" she said, looking up at him. He must have had an expression that confirmed it was indeed her song, for she burst out crying. "Why, my love, why?"

The pain in her voice touched his heart, and he wanted to hug her, to wipe off her tears and tell her everything would be alright. He fought hard with himself, aware that she was in his head, manipulating him. He clutched the brush so tight that blood stopped flowing.

"The story wasn't working," he said. "The song wasn't good. I'll start all over."

It, partly, was the truth. He would have recreated the story again, only to burn it up, and then recreate, over and over again, until he would finally forget her.

She slowly stood up, a smile flickering on her lips. She wiped off the tears with the back of her hand and he thought she was the most beautiful thing he had ever seen in lamplight. He wanted to draw her, to preserve this moment.

She's enchanting you! A voice whispered. *Fight her.*

"I know you love me," she said, taking a hesitant step forward, and he felt a warmth wrap him. The coldness mysteriously vanished. "You loved me at first sight, and you'll love me to the end of time."

This was the happily ever after ending he had searched for all his life. He could see it, even though she was a yamo, she loved him. She had fallen truly in love with him. She would not eat his imagination. She would spare him. Just like in the story, the yamo spared the hero because it loved him. This is it, his happiness. He would grow old with her, and she would fill him with happiness.

She took off the feather blanket, slowly, teasing, and it slid to the floor. Now she stood naked, her skin the colour of fire, her small breasts pointing at him. She had a ring on her navel, beads on her waist, and her ribs showed on her chest like some kind of jewellery. She walked to him, as if in slow motion, and he could feel the heat of her body. This was the moment he had waited for all his life, when he would kiss a woman for the first time, a woman he loved and who loved him back. The moment he would make love for the first time, when his happiness would begin. His lonely days were over.

Except, he was a future kwaro of love. He was destined for loneliness.

He felt the brush slip off his hand, but someone, a part of him that had burned the story, instructed his fingers to keep a tighter grip.

She reached him, after what seemed like an eternity, and wrapped her arms around him. He shuddered. He felt every pore on her naked body, and she smelled oh so good. Her cheek touched his cheek. Fire. That was the only thing he was aware of. Her cheek. Not her breasts, not her arms wound around his shoulders, not her wet vagina. Her cheek. It felt like a lump of burning coal on his skin and he knew it would keep the coldness away. He closed his eyes. He did not want that feeling to ever go away.

"Thank you for loving me the way you do," she whispered.

And he wanted to cry in happiness.

The brush was cold in his palm.

He felt her cheeks leaving his, but the burning sensation continued, and now he felt her lips on his. If her cheek was a lump of coal, then her lips were a furnace. Not human lips.

No way. They were lips of a goddess. His goddess.

Except, he was destined for loneliness.

He stabbed her in the chest, right between her ribs, searching for her heart.

She gasped in shock, and he could feel the enchantment she had cast over him ebb away. The warmth, the heat of her body, the sensation that he had found what he was looking for, all fizzled away, and the coldness hit him as if a block of ice had fallen on him. Her blood squirted. It had a bluish tint. He stabbed her again, and again, and she fell to her knees, groaning, drowning in her own blood, and he stabbed, and stabbed, and her blood soaked his hand like a strange kind of paint.

She sprawled onto the floor, vomiting blood, several holes spewing blood from her chest like fountains. Her eyes now looked like pools of molten metal. Something like a strand of hair sprouted on her chin, twitching and twisting, like a panicked parasite trying to escape the dying body. Hair sprout on her upper lip like the moustache of a clown, and on the sides of her face like a thousand maggots. Tentacles, he realised, tiny hair-like tentacles. Her face dissolved from that of a beautiful young woman, to something that looked like a fish with a beard. She was trying to say something, but there was too much blood in her mouth, and she gurgled, and she twisted on the floor in agony.

He stood over her until she lay still, and the light went out of her eyes.

*

He got out of the hut shortly before dawn, with her feather blanket wrapped tight, pulled over his head like a hood to hide his face. He left his easel, though he cherished it, for the guards would see through the disguise if he tried to take it away. He had to escape before sunrise, when the keeper would come on his daily visit, maybe to gloat that Jamaaro should now hasten with the story.

He hesitated outside the door. Two guards were at the entrance of a nearby hut, sharing a smoking pipe. Then, one looked toward his hut, and whispered something to the other, and in terror they both fled into the hut and shut the door. A moment later, a window opened and one of them peeped out, but, on seeing him staring at them, ducked back inside.

Jamaaro was not too puzzled. They knew about her and were probably terrified that she would put them under her spell. He hurried toward the gate, hoping they would not notice his gait, that the darkness would protect him. Another guard watched the gate but, on seeing him approach, quickly pulled a lever and then fled out of sight. The gate was the sculpture of a hammerkop's head and to open its lower beak dropped to the ground with a rattle of chains. Jamaaro walked out.

He quickened his pace to the nearest boma. It did not have a gate, but a night watchman dozed at the entrance. He woke up as Jamaaro passed him.

"Who is –" he started to ask, but then he saw the feather blanket, and screamed. "Witch!" He fled. He must have heard gossip from the guards down the road.

Jamaaro knew he had only a few moments before the keeper came. He scrambled into a bruka parked near the gate, and pedalled hard and fast.

He jumped into the air just as shouting came from inside the boma. He pedalled harder, desperate, and pulled away from the ground. As he soared, he caught a glimpse of the keeper running ahead of a pack of armed guards racing toward the prison boma. A few moments later he was high above the town, speeding toward the rising sun, just another bruka in the early morning traffic.

Discover Luna Novella in our store:

https://www.lunapresspublishing.com/shop

CPSIA information can be obtained
at www.ICGtesting.com
Printed in the USA
LVHW100725090323
741202LV00004B/562